Josi

Josie and h
and Bun th
exciting sto
include Clic
very naughty mouse, Josie's birthday party and a super holiday at the sea-side . . .

Enid Blyton needs no introduction to her readers. Author of around seven hundred books, which have been translated into almost every language, she has been known and loved by children of all ages for many years.

Enid Blyton titles published by Red Fox
(incorporating Beaver Books)

Josie, Click and Bun and the Little Tree House
Josie, Click and Bun Again
More About Josie, Click and Bun
Five Have a Puzzling Time and Other Stories
The Adventures of Scamp
The Caravan Family
The Christmas Story
The Second Green Goblin Book
Hollow Tree House
The Naughtiest Girl in the School
The Naughtiest Girl Again
The Naughtiest Girl is a Monitor
Tales from Fairyland
More Tales from Fairyland
Three Boys and Circus
Up the Faraway Tree
The Yellow Fairy Book
The Wizard Who Wasn't
The Naughtiest Girl Omnibus (3-in-1)
Adventure Stories (3-in-1)
Animal Stories (3-in-1)
Magic Stories (3-in-1)
The Birthday Kitten/The Boy Who Wanted a Dog (2-in-1)
Mr Twiddle Stories (2-in-1)

MORE ABOUT JOSIE, CLICK AND BUN

Enid Blyton

Illustrated by Dorothy M. Wheeler

RED FOX

A Red Fox Book

Published by Random House Children's Books
20 Vauxhall Bridge Road, London SW1V 2SA

A division of Random House UK Ltd
London Melbourne Sydney Auckland
Johannesburg and agencies throughout the world

3 5 7 9 10 8 6 4 2

First published by George Newnes Limited 1947

Red Fox edition 1996

Set in Great Britain by SX Composing DTP,
Rayleigh, Essex
Printed and bound in Great Britain by
Cox & Wyman Ltd, Reading, Berkshire

RANDOM HOUSE UK Limited Reg. No. 954009

Papers used by Random House UK Ltd are
natural, recyclable products made from wood
grown in sustainable forests. The manufacturing
processes conform to the environmental
regulations of the country of origin.

ISBN 0 09 937191 X

Click At The Party!

Once Click was asked out to a party. Josie dressed him in his very best bow, and brushed out his whiskers.

'Now be a good mouse, and don't be greedy at tea time, and be sure to say "Thank you for having me",' said Josie. 'Goodbye.'

Click had a lovely time at the party. They played musical chairs, and he won.

But oh, what a pity, his balloon burst, and he wept a big puddle of tears. Then another mouse gave Click *his* balloon to cheer him up!

Click told Josie about the kind mouse who had given him his balloon. 'You must ask him to tea,' said Josie.

So Tailie mouse came to tea. Josie was rather cross because he ate the candles out of the candlesticks.

'They are not for tea,' she said. 'That is not good manners. Click, don't giggle. I don't think it's funny to eat my candles.'

But Click thought it was very funny, and he and Tailie became good friends and went out together every day.

Tailie was a naughty mouse. Click was usually a good little thing, but when he was with Tailie he got naughty too.

They went to Mrs Biscuit, the grocer, and Tailie showed Click a big sack with a little hole at the bottom.

'Let's nibble the hole bigger and see what comes out,' he said. So they did, and a lot of white flour trickled out.

'Flour is good to eat,' said Tailie. 'Let's eat it.' So they ate some, and soon Click was covered in white.

Suddenly Tailie heard a noise. 'Someone's coming !' he cried. 'Quick, run!' So they ran away fast.

But they left a white trail behind them, and Mrs Biscuit saw it. She followed it carefully and . . .

. . . it led her to Josie's house! She knocked at the door, and Josie answered it. 'You have a little robber here,' said Mrs Biscuit sternly.

'Oh no,' said Josie, surprised. But Mrs Biscuit pointed to the white trail of flour on the floor. 'Where is Click?' she said.

'Click! Click! Where are you hiding?' called Josie. But Click didn't come. He was hiding under his bed. He was frightened.

'I can see his tail sticking out from under the bed,' said Mrs Biscuit, and she pulled hard at the tail.

Click was pulled out backwards. 'He stole the flour out of my sack,' said Mrs Biscuit. 'I had better tell the policeman.'

'Oh, no, no!' said poor Josie. 'He is only a baby mouse. He didn't know he was doing wrong. Please forgive him, Mrs Biscuit.'

Mrs Biscuit forgave Click just that once. Josie scolded him and so did Bun. They wouldn't let him have any sweets for a whole week.

Click was sad. He wouldn't look at Tailie when he met him. But Tailie linked tails with him and laughed.

'Don't be a silly mouse,' he said. 'You come along with me. I've found something good.'

Click was silly. He went off with Tailie again – but Tailie was so funny, and such a jolly friend. 'You come and see what I've found,' he said.

Tailie took Click through a hole under a house wall. He found himself in a big kitchen. 'Plenty to eat here!' said Tailie.

Tailie found a bit of cheese. Click found something large and yellow. It was soap.

Click bit a piece out and chewed it. It didn't taste very nice. He sneezed and suddenly an enormous soap bubble came out of his mouth.

Click stared at it in alarm. 'I'm bubbling,' he said to Tailie. 'Oh, there's another bubble. Oh, Tailie, what's happening?'

Click was so frightened that he ran home, bubbles coming out of his mouth as he panted and puffed.

He burst into Josie's house. 'Josie, something's wrong with me!' he said, and tears fell down his nose. That made the bubbles worse.

Soon the room was quite full of big soap bubbles. Josie and Bun stared at Click in surprise. 'Stop!' said Josie.

But Click couldn't stop. Out of his mouth came bubbles as big as balloons, and they floated in the air until they burst.

Click Gets Spanked!

'Click,' said Josie, sternly, 'have you been eating soap? Where have you been?'

Click cried and told Josie. 'You are a very naughty mouse,' said Bun. 'We told you not to go with Tailie. It is wrong to nibble other people's soap.'

'I'm afraid Click must be spanked,' said Josie sadly. 'It is the only thing that will teach him. Where is that old slipper of yours, Bun?'

So Bun spanked Click, and Click was so miserable that he promised faithfully he wouldn't go out to play with such a bad friend as Tailie again.

Now, after Click had been spanked, he met Tailie again. 'I've found some bacon rind,' said Tailie. 'Come with me.'

But Click remembered his promises and his spanking, and he wouldn't go. He was a good little mouse that day.

So Tailie went alone – and, oh dear, that bacon rind was in a trap, and while Tailie was nibbling it . . .

. . . the trap went off and he was caught. 'Now you see what happens to bad mice,' said Josie. 'It's a good thing Bun spanked you, or you might have been caught too, Click.'

'Bun, it's Josie's birthday soon,' said Click one day. 'What shall we buy for her? Let's look in our money-boxes.'

'Josie wants a new umbrella,' said Bun. 'And she wants a new thimble too, Click. We haven't got enough money. We must earn some.'

So Bun went to Mrs Biscuit's and got a job at sweeping out the shop – but he did it so well . . .

. . . that he swept over a whole line of customers too! Mrs Biscuit told him to put down the broom and dust the tins on the top shelves.

So Bun took a ladder and climbed up to dust the top shelves. There were hundreds of tins there. Bun looked inside one . . .

. . . but it was full of pepper and when he sniffed into it the pepper got up his nose and made him sneeze.

He fell off the ladder, with tins falling all around him. The tin of pepper spilt into the air, and all the customers . . .

. . . began to sneeze too. Oh, what a sneezing there was! A-tish-oo, a-tish-oo, a-tish-oo!

'I'm sorry,' said Bun, when everyone had stopped sneezing. 'It was the pepper. I'll stay behind tonight and do extra work to make up for this.'

So he did, and he tidied everything beautifully. You should have seen all the soap built up like bricks, and tins in piles, and packets arranged in rows!

'Well you certainly are a good worker,' said Mrs Biscuit at the end of the week. 'Here are your wages.'

Bun was pleased. He put the money in his money-box. Click had some to put in, too. 'Where did you get it?' said Bun.

Click had found some work to do after school. He had gone to Mr Mixem's the chemist, and had said he would deliver his bottles of medicine.

So Mr Mixem gave him six bottles to take round. He told him which bottle was to go to which customer. So Click set off with the bottles tied on his back.

But halfway there they slipped off on to the grass. They didn't break, which was lucky. But they had got mixed up and . . .

. . . Click didn't know which was which. But he made a guess and delivered them all. But alas, some went to the wrong people!

When Click went back to tell Mr Mixem that the bottles had got mixed up, and he was afraid that he had taken them to the wrong people . . .

Mr Mixem groaned and said, 'Now we *shall* get into trouble! Moudie Mole will take Reggie Rat's medicine, and . . .

. . . Bertie Badger will take Harry Hedgehog's. There will be a lot of complaints tomorrow, Click. I shan't pay you any money for your work.'

But would you believe it, everyone went to Mr Mixem to say that the medicine had done them more good than usual – so Click got his pennies after all!

'I shall go and buy Josie an umbrella now,' said Bun. 'And you can go and get her a thimble. Take her old one, Click, for the size.'

So they set off together. Bun went to the umbrella shop and bought a lovely umbrella. It was blue and red.

Click opened it, but he didn't open it properly, and it suddenly shut itself down on him!

Oh dear, Click was so frightened that he ran out of the shop with the umbrella shut on him. He had only his back legs to run with!

'Stop! Stop!' yelled Bun. 'You will spoil that umbrella! Stop!' But Click didn't stop. He knocked over a lot of people . . .

. . . and then he came to a pond. He didn't see where he was going and he fell right in!

But luckily the umbrella opened itself again, and Click found himself floating safely inside it, like a funny boat!

He floated right into the middle of some ducks. 'Quack!' they said in fright. They pecked at the umbrella, and it rocked to and fro.

Click was right in the middle of the pond, with the ducks pecking at his umbrella boat. Bun got a rope and threw it . . .

. . . and it caught on the points of the umbrella. Then Bun drew it safely to shore. He was cross with Click.

'What silly behaviour!' he said. 'Do you want me to spank you again? I will if you have spoilt this umbrella.'

But wasn't it lucky, the umbrella wasn't a bit spoilt, so Click didn't get spanked. It began to rain, and he and Bun went home under the new umbrella.

Then Click wanted to buy a thimble for Josie's birthday. So he went to a shop that sold all kinds of thimbles. . . .

. . . and he bought a beautiful one, just the size of Josie's old one. The shop girl measured them to see.

On the way home Click stumbled over a stone and dropped the new thimble. It rolled away and away . . .

. . . and when Click looked for it he couldn't find it anywhere. 'It went down that hole,' said a mouse. 'That's where Tiny One, the pixie lives.'

Click called down the hole, 'Tiny One! Are you there? I want to speak to you.'

Tiny One called back, 'Yes, I'm here. I can't come. I'm trying on a new hat.'

'Well, I'm coming down to you if you won't come up to me,' said Click; and down the hole he went.

And would you believe it, Tiny One's new hat was the silver thimble that Click had bought for Josie! Just see!

'Tiny One! That's not a new hat for you. That's a silver thimble I bought for Josie,' said Click crossly.

'Well, I like it,' said Tiny One. 'I shall keep it. It's the nicest hat I've ever had. I shall put ribbon round it. Look!'

'Oh, please, do let me have it,' said Click. Tiny One looked sad. 'It's *so* nice,' she said, 'I've never had one like it before.'

'Well, you have *this* one,' said Click suddenly, and he held out Josie's old thimble. 'It's just the same.' So Tiny One had the old thimble and Click ran off with the new one.

'We must give a party for Josie,' said Bun. 'We will ask Jolly, the sailor doll, and Tiptoe, the fairy doll, because they are Josie's friends.'

'And Big-Ears, the pixie and Amelia Jane, the naughty doll,' said Click. Josie was pleased to think she would have a party.

She sent Click and Bun to ask the guests to come. Everyone was very pleased. 'You must try to be good for once, Amelia Jane,' said Tiptoe.

Josie began to make cakes and jellies and sandwiches. There were piles and piles of them. They made Click feel very hungry.

Josie Gets Her Presents!

Josie had a new dress for her party. It was all frills and she looked sweet in it. She wore a new bow in her hair, too.

Bun gave her the umbrella. She was so pleased with it. 'Just what I wanted!' she said.

Then Click gave her the thimble and told her how he had had to give her old one to Tiny One for a hat.

'I wondered where it had gone to!' said Josie, kissing Click. 'It is a lovely present, and I shall put it on when I darn your bed-socks!'

Everyone came to the party together. Jolly and Tiptoe brought flowers for Josie, and Big-Ears brought perfume.

Amelia Jane brought a little musical box. She set it going whilst they had tea. It made Click want to dance.

There was a birthday cake with candles on. Bun lighted them. The cake looked so pretty.

There were crackers with paper hats in, and balloons afterwards. Amelia Jane was naughty and burst Bun's balloon.

'Now, Amelia Jane,' said Big-Ears the pixie, 'give Bun *your* balloon instead. Why must you always be naughty?'

But everyone forgot about Amelia Jane's naughtiness when the musical box began to play again. They got up and danced.

There was no one to dance with Click. He felt sad and hid in a corner. 'Where's Click?' called Josie.

'You dance us your sailor dance that you got a prize for at school,' said Josie. So Click did, and he was clapped and felt very happy.

Click went to school each day. He was supposed to take a hanky with him, and Josie always gave him one.

But he somehow lost it on the way to school, and Mr Rap was cross with him. So was Josie.

Then one day she had a good idea. 'I shall tie it in a knot round your tail,' she said. 'Then, if you lose your hanky, you will lose your tail, too!'

And after that Click always arrived at school with a clean hanky. But how everyone laughed at him!

One day Kiddle, a baby goat, came to Mr Rap's school. He was a dear little thing. He sat next to Click.

He was rather stupid, Click thought, and he was always hungry. If Click wasn't careful Kiddle would eat every bit of Click's lunch in one gobble.

So Click and the others kept their lunches locked up in their desks. Kiddle didn't know how to unlock them, so that was good.

Then things began to disappear. First Click's rubber went, and then his best pencil. Then all his books disappeared, and he was very upset.

Things went on disappearing in a most peculiar way at Mr Rap's school. Johnny Mole's mackintosh went. Click's hat went.

Then a pile of books that Mr Rap had left on a table disappeared too. And then Mr Rap's cane went! Everybody was glad about that, of course.

'What is happening to everything?' said Click. And then they found out! It was Kiddle, the baby goat. He had eaten the books and the mackintosh and the hat – everything!

As he had eaten Mr Rap's cane, he couldn't be spanked. But he was sent home to his mother, and she butted him so hard that he cried for a whole day.

Click Goes Out To Tea!

Kiddle, the goat-baby, didn't come to school any more. But Mr Rap took a new pupil – a kitten called Whiskers.

Click loved Whiskers. He took him home to tea with him and the others liked him too. He had very good manners.

'Thank you for a nice tea,' he said to Josie. 'And please may Click come to tea with me tomorrow?'

So the next day Click set off to go to tea with Whiskers. He had a new bow on his tail and felt very happy.

But dear me, when he got to Whiskers's home, he found that Whiskers's mother was a big black cat . . .

. . . and Whiskers's father was a big ginger cat, and Whiskers's granny was a tabby. They were all dressed very nicely.

And there was a nice tea. But Click couldn't help feeling very uncomfortable. They stared at him so, and . . .

. . . suddenly the old tabby granny said in a loud whisper, 'He's nice and fat, isn't he? Oh, very nice and fat!'

'I think I'd better go home now,' said Click, after a while. 'Oh, no, you can't go yet,' said Whiskers's mother.

'We like mice,' said Whiskers, and he smiled a horrid smile. When Click ran to the door, it was locked!

Now Josie and Bun had a friend to tea that day. It was Big-Ears the pixie. 'Where's Click?' he said.

When Josie told him, he was alarmed. 'But Whiskers's people are *cats*,' he said, and Click is a mouse! How *could* you let him go there?'

Well, Josie was upset when she heard what Big-Ears said about Click having gone to tea with a family of cats. She jumped up.

She and Bun ran all the way to Whiskers's home. They rapped on the door. They could hear poor Click squeaking away inside.

'They won't let us in if they know it's us,' said Bun. 'We'll play a trick.' He banged again. 'We've come for the washing!' he cried.

So the cat family opened the door – and Josie and Bun rushed in to get Click. How glad he was see them!

'We shall never let you go out to tea with a cat family again,' said Josie, when she put Click to bed that day.

'Choose better friends,' said Bun. 'First you choose Tailie, who was naughty. Then you choose Whiskers, who will grow into a cat.'

So Click chose another friend. He chose a large green caterpillar, with tufts of red fur on its back!

Josie didn't much like caterpillars, but Crawler seemed polite and quiet and good, though he was always eating.

Crawler and Click played together a lot. They played Red Indians and wore hats made of feathers. The caterpillar looked funny.

They played hide-and-seek, but Crawler always munched leaves when he hid, and so Click found him easily because he could hear him.

Then, one day, Crawler didn't want to play. 'I don't feel well,' he said. 'You've eaten too much,' said Click. 'Yes, I feel I'm going to burst,' said Crawler.

And, oh dear, he did burst – out of his skin! It split down his back. Click ran crying to Josie. 'Come quick! Crawler's burst!'

Josie ran to help. But dear me, what a surprise for her! Crawler was creeping right out of his old skin, and underneath . . .

. . . he had a new one, looser for him than the old one! 'It's not a very polite thing to do, really,' said Josie. 'Click, I hope you won't copy Crawler in this.'

One day Crawler did something queer. He made himself a brown case and went to sleep in it. Click couldn't wake him up.

'He's no fun now,' said Click. And then one day a surprising thing happened. The case split open . . .

. . . And out came a great big butterfly! Click ran crying to Josie again. 'Josie, Josie! Crawler wasn't inside that case after all!'

The big butterfly dried his crinkled wings and flew down beside Click. 'Don't be afraid!' he said.

'I was Crawler once – but now I've changed into a big butterfly. Come for a ride on my back, little mouse.'

So Click went for a ride on the butterfly's back – and oh, how he loved it!

Well, when Click saw that Crawler had grown wings when he went to sleep in a little brown case . . .

. . . he made himself a case out of wood, and crawled into it to sleep. 'I shall wake up with wings,' he said.

But he didn't. It was very sad. He had just his tail and whiskers, but no wings. But Josie was glad.

'If you had wings you would fly off and leave us,'she said. 'We couldn't do without you, Click. Here's a penny to buy some sweets. Cheer up!'

Once Bun found a bag of carrots in the road. He picked it up and ran home in delight. He began to eat them and he gave one to Click.

But when Josie came home, how cross she was! 'How dare you eat those carrots!' she cried. 'They are not yours.'

'They are Neddy's the donkey. Take them back to him at once and say you are sorry for eating some. I am ashamed of you.'

Bun and Click were cross. They took the carrots back to Neddy and when he heard they had eaten some, he nipped Bun's ears and Click's tail.

Bun Gets His Purse Back!

Bun wished he hadn't taken the carrots back to Neddy. On the way home he lost his purse full of money! He was very sad.

'Oh, Josie, I've lost my purse!' he said. 'I can't buy a new hat now, nor that walking-stick for Click. Oh, I do hope someone will bring my purse back.'

'Maybe they will take it home and keep it, as you did Neddy's carrots,' said Josie. 'It would serve you right.'

But little Harry Hedgehog brought back the purse, and Bun was so pleased. 'You dear, honest fellow!' he said. 'You make me feel ashamed of taking Neddy's carrots!'

Bun was so sorry he had taken Neddy's carrots that he planted carrot seeds to grow some for Neddy.

'Why are you planting those?' said Click. 'Well, I shall plant something, too. I would like things to grow for me.'

So Click got some crumbs of cheese and a few bits of bacon rind, and he planted them in his garden.

'Now I shall soon have cheese and bacon growing up to give Josie!' he said. But, oh, what a pity, his seeds didn't grow, and he was very sad!

Bun Is Very Ill!

One day Bun ate something that gave him a pain. He had to go to bed, and Josie looked after him.

Soon the doctor came and felt his pulse. 'Very hot,' he said. 'Keep him quiet. Give him ice-cream and jelly to eat.'

But poor Bun was too ill to eat even ice-cream or jelly. So Click ate them up, and Josie said he would soon go to bed too, if he ate so much.

People came to visit Bun, and brought him books to read, and grapes to eat, and lemonade to drink. But he didn't seem to get better at all.

'I think Bun had better go away to the seaside,' said the doctor at last. 'Pack up everything, and take him away, Josie.'

'It would be nice to have a house by the sea,' said Josie. Bun agreed, so she decided to go to the seaside for the day and look round.

Next day she asked Moudie Mole to keep an eye on Bun. Then she and Click took the train to Sunnybanks.

The house agent had just the little house they wanted. It was very comfortably furnished.

When they got home they found Bun eating some chicken broth Moudie Mole had made for him. He was feeling a lot better.

Then Josie packed up all the clothes they would need for a long stay by the sea. Click helped her.

They asked Big-Ears the pixie to lend them his car, because Bun wasn't well enough to go by train.

They asked Moudie Mole to look after their house for them whilst they were away, and gave her the key.

And then one day Big-Ears came round with his car, and went indoors to fetch Bun.

He carried him into the car, and piled him up with cushions and rugs. Everyone got in with the luggage.

Then off they went to the seaside. Big-Ears drove very carefully.

Bun went to bed at once with a glass of hot milk and some biscuits.

Next day Bun felt well enough to get up. He was very pleased with the house Josie had chosen.

There was a nice garden, too, with flowers and fruit trees.

They found some gardening tools in the shed, and Bun and Click said they would do some gardening.

And Bun already feels much better, and they are all having the loveliest holiday they have ever had in their lives!